honorary member

The
Cool Crazy Crickets

THE COOL CRAZY CRICKETS
To THE Rescue!

David Elliott

ILLUSTRATED BY Paul Meisel

CANDLEWICK PRESS

For Richard Sweeney, who rescues more than cats
D. E.

For Myril Adler, a great teacher
P. M.

Text copyright © 2001 by David Elliott
Illustrations copyright © 2001 by Paul Meisel

First paperback edition in this format 2010

The Library of Congress has cataloged the hardcover edition as follows:

Elliott, David (David A.)
The Cool Crazy Crickets to the rescue! / David Elliott ; illustrated by Paul Meisel.
— 1st ed.
p.   cm.
Summary: The members of the Cool Crazy Crickets club decide to earn some
money, but they have differences of opinion about how they should spend it.
ISBN 978-0-7636-1116-3 (hardcover)
[1. Clubs — Fiction. 2. Moneymaking projects — Fiction.]
I. Meisel, Paul, ill. II. Title.
PZ7.E447 Cp 2001
[Fic] — dc21 00-020775
ISBN 978-0-7636-1402-7 (paperback)
ISBN 978-0-7636-4658-5 (reformatted paperback)

10 11 12 13 14 15 16 CCP 10 9 8 7 6 5 4 3 2 1

Printed in Shenzhen, Guangdong, China

This book was typeset in Usherwood and Tempus Sans.
The illustrations were done in watercolor and ink.

Candlewick Press
99 Dover Street
Somerville, Massachusetts 02144

visit us at www.candlewick.com

CONTENTS

CHAPTER 1

No Dues!

A shaggy little dog walked down the street. It was Noodles, the mascot of the club known as the Cool Crazy Crickets.

Noodles was just thinking how happy he was to be a mascot when the Crickets themselves came running around the corner.

"Noodles!" said Leo. "There you are!"

"We've been looking all over for you," said Phoebe.

"We want to play follow-the-leader," said Miranda.

"And we want *you* to be the leader," Marcus added.

Noodles had always wanted to be a leader. He ran around the Crickets' clubhouse. The Crickets ran around their clubhouse.

Noodles rolled on his back. The Crickets rolled on their backs.

Noodles scratched his ear. The Crickets scratched their ears.

Suddenly, Noodles stopped
scratching and started growling.
A dirty, one-eyed cat
rounded the corner.
Its tail was crooked.
Its whiskers were
bent. Its ears were torn and jagged.

"Oh, no!" yelled Miranda. "It's *that
cat*!"

No one knew where the one-eyed cat
came from. No one knew where the
one-eyed cat slept. The one-eyed cat
was a *stray*.

"My mom said that cat might *bite*,"
said Miranda.

"My mom said that cat might
scratch," said Marcus.

"My mom said that cat might bite *and*
scratch," said Phoebe.

"Run!" shouted Leo. "Run for your
lives!"

The Cool Crazy Crickets took off as fast as they could. Noodles took off after the one-eyed cat. No stray was going to bite the Cool Crazy Crickets! He would make sure of that!

But being a stray had taught the one-eyed cat many things. And escaping from shaggy mascots was one of them.

The Cool Crazy Crickets stopped running when they got to Mr. Lee's store.

"I need a snack," said Marcus.

"Me, too," said Phoebe. "Running makes you hungry."

There were lots of good snacks in Mr. Lee's store.

"Chocolate!" said Marcus.

"Chips!" said Phoebe.

"Ice cream!" said Miranda.

"Cookies!" said Leo.

"Three dollars and fifty cents!" said Mr. Lee.

Leo looked at Miranda. Marcus looked
at Phoebe.

Phoebe didn't look at anyone. "I
would pay for the snacks," she said,
"except for one thing."

"What's that?" asked Leo.

"I don't have any money," Phoebe
replied.

The Cool Crazy Crickets
returned their snacks
to the shelves.

"I thought you were in a club," said Mr. Lee. "Doesn't it have dues?"

"What are dues?" Marcus asked. "Can you eat them?"

"No, you can't eat them," said Mr. Lee. "Dues are money that members pay to be in a club."

"No dues!" Marcus shouted.

"Right!" Miranda agreed. "Dues are out!"

"Let's *make* money, then," said Leo.

"Okay," said Phoebe. "I'll get the paper and the scissors."

"I don't mean *that*," said Leo. "I mean let's *earn* money. Lots of clubs earn money."

"But how?" asked Marcus. "How can the Cool Crazy Crickets earn money?"

"We could try baby-sitting," said Leo.

"And we could try pet-sitting," Miranda added.

"And we could try a lemonade stand," said Phoebe.

"Those are good ideas," said Mr. Lee. "And you can advertise them right here in my store."

Later that afternoon, the Cool Crazy Crickets were making posters to hang in Mr. Lee's window.

"I'm glad we don't have dues," said Marcus.

"Me, too," said Phoebe. "Dues are dumb."

Suddenly, Leo started laughing.

"What's so funny?" asked Miranda.

"I was just thinking about Miss Fein," said Leo.

"Our teacher?" asked Miranda. "What's so funny about Miss Fein?"

"Well," said Leo. "Remember how she used to talk about *do*'s and *don't*'s?"

"Sure," said Phoebe. "The things you're supposed to do are called *do*'s."

"And the things you're not supposed to do are called *don't*'s," Marcus added.

"So?" said Miranda. "What's so funny about *do's* and *don't's?*"

"Well," said Leo. "Instead of *do's* and *don't's* . . . the Cool Crazy Crickets *don't's* have *dues!*"

"Hey, Noodles!" said Marcus. "Did you hear that? The Cool Crazy Crickets *don't*'s have *dues*!"

But Noodles hadn't heard a thing. He was too busy dreaming that he had caught the one-eyed cat at last.

CHAPTER 2

Baby-sitting Is Easy

The next day, Leo, Miranda, and
Phoebe were at their clubhouse.
Marcus came running down the street.

"Guess what!" he shouted. "We have
a job!"

"A job?" asked Leo. "What kind
of job?"

"Baby-sitting!" Marcus answered. "It's a baby-sitting job!"

"Who are we baby-sitting for?" asked Phoebe.

Marcus looked up at the sky. His face turned red. He started to whistle.

"Oh, no!" Miranda shouted. "It's your little brother *Teddy,* isn't it!"

That afternoon, the Cool Crazy
Crickets met at Marcus's house.

"I'm taking our goldfish, Finny, to see
Dr. Vega," said Marcus's mother, as she
stepped out the door. "I'll be back in an
hour. Teddy is taking a nap. Try not to
wake him."

From upstairs came the sound of two little feet hitting the floor.

"Oh, no," said Phoebe. "He's awake."

"I have an idea," said Leo. "Let's take turns baby-sitting Teddy. Each Cricket will watch him for fifteen minutes."

"The rest of us can wait outside on the porch," said Miranda. "Where it's safe."

"Who'll go first?" asked Marcus.

"That's easy," said Leo. "I'm thinking of a number between one and ten. Whoever guesses the number will go first."

"Okay," said Phoebe. "Three."

"You win!" said Leo. And he ran out the door with Miranda and Marcus.

Phoebe was alone . . . alone with TEDDY!

"PLAY!" Teddy shouted. "PLAY TAND-UP-IT-DOWN!"

"Tand up it down?" Phoebe said.

"IT DOWN!" Teddy yelled as he sat down on the floor.

"Oh," said Phoebe, sitting down next to Teddy. "I get it. *Sit down.*"

"TAND UP!" Teddy shouted as he stood up.

"Stand up?" Phoebe said. "But I just sat down."

Fifteen minutes later, Miranda came in. Teddy and Phoebe were *still* standing up and sitting down.

"Help!" Phoebe cried. "My legs feel like spaghetti!"

"Hello, Teddy," Miranda said.
"My name is Miranda."

"MIRANDA HORSIE!" Teddy said.

"Not Miranda Horsie," said Miranda.
"Just plain Miranda."

"MIRANDA HORSIE!" Teddy shouted.
"GIDDEEUP!"

Fifteen minutes later, Leo came in.

"Help!" Miranda begged. "Help! He won't get off!"

Leo lifted Teddy from Miranda's back. She ran out to the porch.

"WHERE MIRANDA HORSIE GO?" Teddy asked. A tear slowly rolled down his cheek.

"Oh, no!" said Leo. "No, Teddy! Please don't cry!"

"WAAAAAAAAAH!"

"Marcus!" yelled Leo. "Help me! What should I do?"

"Make funny faces. He likes that," said Marcus through the screen door.

Leo crossed his eyes and scrunched up his nose. He raised his eyebrows and puffed up his cheeks. He stuck out his tongue and waggled his ears.

"WAAAAAAAH!" Teddy screamed louder than ever. "WAAAH! WAAAAAAAAAAH!"

"I said make *funny* faces," Marcus yelled from the porch. "Not *scary* faces!"

Ten minutes later, Marcus's mother stepped up onto the porch.

"Dr. Vega said Finny is going to be fine," said Marcus's mother. "How is Teddy?"

"TEDDY PLAY TAND-UP-IT-DOWN!" shouted Teddy. "TEDDY PLAY HORSIE!" Marcus's mother gave Teddy a big kiss. She gave the Crickets three dollars.

"Baby-sitting is easy!" said Marcus. "We should do it again!"

"Next time," said Phoebe, "*you're* going first!"

CHAPTER 3

A Tiny Job

The next morning, the Cool Crazy
Crickets were discussing what to do
with the money they had earned.

"Snacks!" said Marcus. "Let's
buy lots and lots of snacks!"

 "A periscope," said Leo.
"To keep an eye out for that cat."

"Art supplies," said Miranda.
"Paints and crayons and paper."

"A camera," said Phoebe. "So we can
take funny pictures."

29

Suddenly, Noodles sat up and barked. Noodles wasn't just a mascot. He was also a watchdog.

"Excuse me," said a voice from outside the clubhouse.

Leo looked out the peephole. "It's a *lady*," he whispered to the Crickets.

Noodles stopped barking. He went outside and licked the lady's hand. Leo followed Noodles outside.

"My name is Mrs. Smith," the lady said. "I'm looking for the Cool Crazy Crickets."

Phoebe stuck her head out the door. "*We're* the Cool Crazy Crickets," she said.

"I saw your signs in Mr. Lee's store,"
Mrs. Smith said. "Can you pet-sit
for Tiny?"

"Who's Tiny?" asked Marcus.

"My puppy," said Mrs. Smith. "He's
very sweet."

An hour later, the Cool Crazy Crickets were standing on Mrs. Smith's porch.

"Pet-sitting for a puppy should be easy," said Miranda.

"Especially if his name is Tiny," said Phoebe.

Leo rang the doorbell.

"Cool Crazy Crickets," said Mrs. Smith. "Meet Tiny!"

"That's not a puppy!" said Phoebe. "That's a pony!"

"Tiny is an Irish wolfhound," said Mrs. Smith. "He's one year old."

"Hello, Tiny," said Leo. Tiny gave Leo a huge kiss.

34

"There is one thing that you should know," said Mrs. Smith. "Tiny is afraid of cats."

"The only cat Tiny should be afraid of is a lion!" said Phoebe.

"It's just *one* cat, really," Mrs. Smith whispered. "Everything should be fine, as long as *that cat* doesn't show up."

After Mrs. Smith left, the Crickets stayed on the porch with Tiny.

"Pet-sitting is much easier than baby-sitting," said Phoebe.

"At least with Tiny I don't have to play HORSIE," said Miranda.

Suddenly, Tiny stood up.

"Oh, no!" said Marcus. "Look!"

It was the one-eyed cat.

"Go away!" yelled Phoebe. "Go away, you bad cat!"

But the cat didn't go away.

Instead, it hopped onto the sidewalk. That's when Tiny began to shiver.

Then the cat hopped onto the porch. That's when Tiny began to cry.

Then the cat hopped onto Tiny! That's when Tiny began to *run*!

"Help!" the Crickets yelled. "Help! Help! Help!"

From out of nowhere, a certain shaggy mascot appeared. The one-eyed cat took one look at Noodles and jumped off Tiny's back. Then it took off as fast as it could.

"Hooray for Noodles!" yelled the Cool Crazy Crickets. "Hooray for our hero, Noodles!"

Later that day, the Cool Crazy Crickets were back in their clubhouse.

"We have three dollars from baby-sitting," said Miranda.

"And four dollars from pet-sitting," said Marcus.

"That makes seven dollars!" said Miranda.

"That's almost enough to buy a periscope," said Leo.

"Snacks!" said Marcus. "I need snacks!"

"What about my paints?" asked Miranda.

"And the camera!" said Phoebe.

Noodles sat in the corner of the clubhouse. He knew that the Cool Crazy Crickets didn't need a periscope. He knew they didn't need snacks, or paints, or a camera. He knew what they did need, though. Dog bones! A wagonful of dog bones! After all, wasn't *he* the hero?

CHAPTER 4

Whose Cat Is It, Anyway?

The next day, the Cool Crazy Crickets set up a lemonade stand. Phoebe and Marcus brought the lemonade. Leo and Miranda brought cookies.

Mr. Lee bought some lemonade.

So did Mrs. Smith.

So did Marcus's mom.

But their best customer was Teddy!
"TEDDY LIKE LEMONADE!" he
shouted. "TEDDY LIKE COOKIES!"
Soon, all the lemonade and cookies
were gone.

"Let's go back to the clubhouse and count our money," said Marcus.

But when the Cool Crazy Crickets got to their clubhouse, something was wrong!

The secret door was open!

The Cool Crazy Crickets crept closer. Miranda peeked in the window.

"Oh, no," she said. "*That cat* is in our clubhouse."

The Cool Crazy Crickets watched as the one-eyed cat lifted its head from the clubhouse floor. It looked at the Crickets and meowed softly. Then it laid its head back down and closed its one good eye.

"Something is wrong," said Miranda.

"It's sick," said Phoebe. "Poor thing."

"We've got to do something," said Leo. "We can't just leave it."

"Even if it is *that cat,*" said Marcus.

Noodles wasn't so sure. Strays could be tricky.

"Let's take it to Dr. Vega," said Leo. "She helped Finny. Maybe she can help a sick cat, too."

The Cool Crazy Crickets wrapped the cat in a blanket. They put it in a wagon. They pulled the wagon to Dr. Vega's office.

"This cat is very sick," said Dr. Vega. "I can help her, but it will be expensive."

"I call a secret meeting of the club," Leo said. The four friends huddled in a corner of Dr. Vega's office.

"We made seven dollars today," said Miranda, after she had counted the money.

"And we already have seven dollars," said Phoebe.

"That makes fourteen dollars," said Leo. "I hope that's enough to make the cat better."

"Me, too," said Phoebe.

"But what about the snacks?" asked Marcus. "What about the periscope and the paints and the camera?"

"What about the poor little one-eyed cat?" Miranda asked.

The Cool Crazy Crickets walked back to Dr. Vega.

"We have fourteen dollars," said Leo. "Is that enough?"

Dr. Vega thought for a moment. "Yes," she said at last. "That will be enough. Come back in a week."

One week later, the Cool Crazy Crickets returned to Dr. Vega's office. The cat still had only one eye. Her tail was still crooked. Her whiskers were still bent. Her ears were still torn and jagged. But now she was clean, and now she was healthy. She was *almost* pretty.

The Cool Crazy Crickets paid Dr. Vega the fourteen dollars they had earned.

"Thank you," said Dr. Vega. "By the way, where are you taking her?"

"To our clubhouse," said Leo. "My dad said we could keep her."

"And that's what we named her," said Phoebe. "*Keeper.*"

"We're going to take good care of her, too," said Miranda proudly.

"But I thought you already *had* a mascot," said Dr. Vega, looking at Noodles.

"We do," said Marcus.

"But we decided that our mascot needs a mascot," said Miranda.

"And that will be Keeper," said Phoebe.

Keeper stuck out her rough tongue and licked Noodles's ear.

Later, the Cool Crazy Crickets told
Mr. Lee the story of Keeper.
"This calls for a celebration," he said.
"Earning money was fun," said Leo.

"But saving Keeper was *more* fun," said Miranda.

And everyone agreed, even Noodles.

He had always wanted his own mascot.

And now he had one . . . even if it was *that cat*.

MIRANDA   LEO
MARCUS   PHOEBE
NOODLES   KEEPER

The Cool Crazy Crickets
to the Rescue!

THE END